For Aglaia, Tassilo, Christoph and Xandi—keep dreaming!
Liz

For Rüdi.
Martina

Copyright © 2005 by Annette Betz Verlag, Vienna, Austria, and Munich, Germany.
First published under the title *Fredo träumt vom Fliegen*.
English translation copyright © 2007 by North-South Books Inc., New York.

First published in the United States, Great Britain, Canada, Australia, and New Zealand in 2007 by
North-South Books Inc., an imprint of NordSüd Verlag AG, Zürich, Switzerland.
Distributed in the United States by North-South Books Inc., New York.

Library of Congress Cataloging-in-Publication Data is available.
A CIP catalogue record for this book is available from The British Library.

ISBN-13: 978-0-7358-2121-7 / ISBN-10: 0-7358-2121-6 (trade edition)
1 3 5 7 9 10 8 6 4 2

Printed in Belgium

Published in cooperation with Annette Betz Verlag, Vienna, Munich

When Donkeys Fly!

By Elisabeth Schöberl
Illustrated by Martina Badstuber

Translated by Helle Martens

NORTHSOUTH
BOOKS
New York / London

Something was wrong with Fred. For hours, the little donkey had been anxiously pacing. Back and forth he went, without looking where he was going. Suddenly—*boom*! He bumped right into Penelope the pig!

"Hey, watch where you're going!" grunted Penelope. "What's bothering you?"

The other animals
wanted to know, too. Suddenly,
everyone was talking at once.

"Silence!" shouted Ronnie the dog,
and everyone was quiet. "All right, Fred,
tell us what's going on."

"I, uh, well, I . . . I have this dream," Fred admitted.
"I want to learn how to fly."

For a minute, no one said anything. Then all the animals looked
at each other and burst out laughing.

"Oh, Fred, you're so silly! Who ever heard of a flying donkey,"
giggled the goat. "That's impossible."

"Anything is possible if you believe in it enough," answered Fred,
feeling hurt. "Don't any of you have dreams?"

The other animals were suddenly quiet.

"I have dreams, too," said Ronnie later, back in the barn. "I want to run faster and bark louder than any other dog."

Rocky the rooster dreamed of being able to sleep in—just for once. Penelope the pig had a dream, too. "There is one thing I wish I could do, but I'm much, much too afraid," she whispered so quietly that no one could hear.

The next morning, Fred finally decided it was time to try to make his dream come true. He stretched out under a tree and studied the birds. It doesn't look that hard, he thought. He practiced flapping his front legs the way the birds flapped their wings. When he thought he had practiced enough, he prepared for his first flight. He squatted down deeply, and then with all his might, he ran hard and leaped up into the air, flapping his legs as fast as he could. But as fast as he went up, he came down again. He crashed and tumbled to the bottom of the hill.

Disappointed, Fred limped back to the farm.

"Donkeys aren't made for flying. But watch me! *My* dream will come true. Farmer Joe's dog will be here any minute. We're going to race to see who can run faster," said Ronnie.

"Okay, you two," said Penelope when Farmer Joe's dog arrived. "On your mark! Get set! Go!" The track went around the barnyard, and Ronnie immediately took the lead.

But before long, he lost his breath, and his opponent flashed by like lightning, beating him by a tail's length.

The next morning, Fred looked up and saw a dragonfly. *Aha! I've got it!* he thought. He ran to the shed, grabbed a few rags and some tools, and started building. What he made looked a bit odd—something between a propeller and an umbrella. At last he was ready. He found a cliff, tied his flying mechanism to his back, and ran as fast as he could. Just before the edge of the cliff, he tucked his legs beneath him and soared through the air. But suddenly a gust of wind came in from one side and pulled him down— *splash!* right into the fishpond.

"When are you going to stop this craziness?"
asked Ronnie, as Fred came back dripping wet.
   "Never," said Fred. "Everything worthwhile takes time. Maybe,
if you practiced every day, you would have won that race."

   "Hrmph,"grunted Ronnie, "I have a better idea!
Farmer Smith's dog and I are going to compete
to see who can bark the loudest."
   "You start, Ronnie," said Penelope. And Ronnie
barked so loudly that everyone covered
their ears.

"Your turn," he said happily to the neighbor's dog. But her bark was so loud that she made two of the hens faint. "Sorry, Ronnie," said Penelope. "But I think it's pretty clear who the winner is!"

Ronnie was so embarrassed, he just wanted to hide in his doghouse.

"At least you tried," said Penelope, comforting him. "I don't even have the guts to try."

"What is your dream?" asked Ronnie.

"I . . . I always wanted to travel," admitted Penelope shyly.

"Well, why don't you?" asked Ronnie.

"Because I'm too scared. I could be attacked by a wolf, or I could get run over by a tractor."

Fred shook his head. "Penelope, you shouldn't be so afraid of everything, and Ronnie, you shouldn't be so lazy."

The next day, Fred tried flying again, but nothing went right.
He lay down sadly in his stall.

"Don't give up, Fred," said Penelope. "You'll find a way, I'm sure. By the way, why do you want to fly so badly?"

"Well, uh, I, well, . . ." Fred stammered, "I just always wanted to soar through the air and see the world from above."

"Hmm . . ." said Penelope, "yes, I can see that you would need to fly to do that."

Suddenly, Ronnie jumped up. "Wait—I have an idea!" he said excitedly. "Follow me!"

Fred and Penelope followed Ronnie to the foot of a tree. "What is *that*?" they shouted, surprised.

Above them in the tree hung a big basket from a long piece of cloth. "That's a balloon. You can fly with it," said Ronnie. "It has been hanging here for weeks. If we can fix it, we can fly it."

"Great idea," said Fred happily, and he and Penelope and Ronnie tugged at the basket until it fell to the ground. Then the three of them worked together to fix the hole in the fabric, blew up the balloon, and secured it to the ground.

"All aboard!" shouted Fred excitedly.

"Oh, you guys go ahead, I'll stay here and watch," said Penelope, looking fearfully at the wobbly thing in front of her.

"But, Penelope, you always wanted to travel. Come on! We'll take good care of you," Fred reassured her, climbing into the basket. Penelope took a deep breath and followed him in. Finally, Ronnie climbed in, too.

The balloon soared up into the air. "We did it!" Fred cheered. "Thanks to you two!"

Penelope grunted happily.

"I know one thing," said Ronnie smiling. "I am flying higher than any dog in the world."

Everyone laughed.

Hours later, when Fred, Penelope, and Ronnie returned from their trip, Rocky the rooster crowed with excitement. The animals couldn't wait to hear about their adventure.

"So, have all of your dreams come true now?" asked the goat.

"Actually," said Fred, "I've always wanted to learn how to ice-skate!"